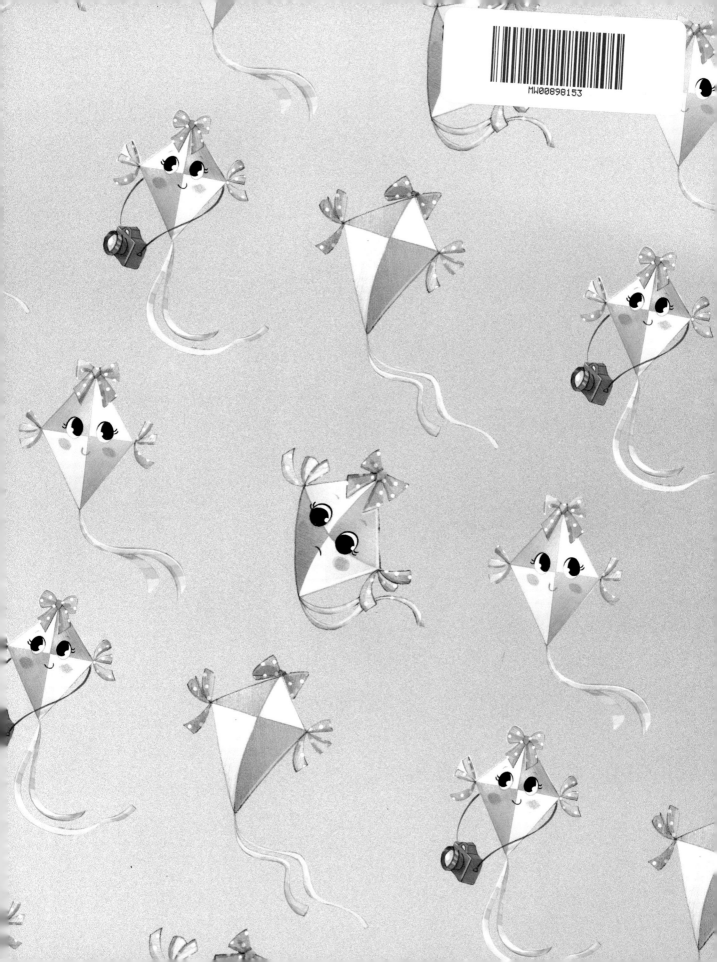

www.mascotbooks.com

Miss Kite Can't Do Right

For more information, please contact:
Mascot Books
620 Herndon Parkway #320
Herndon, VA 20170
info@mascotbooks.com

Library of Congress Control Number: 2021909477
CPSIA Code: PRT0821A
ISBN-13: 978-1-64543-889-2

Printed in the United States

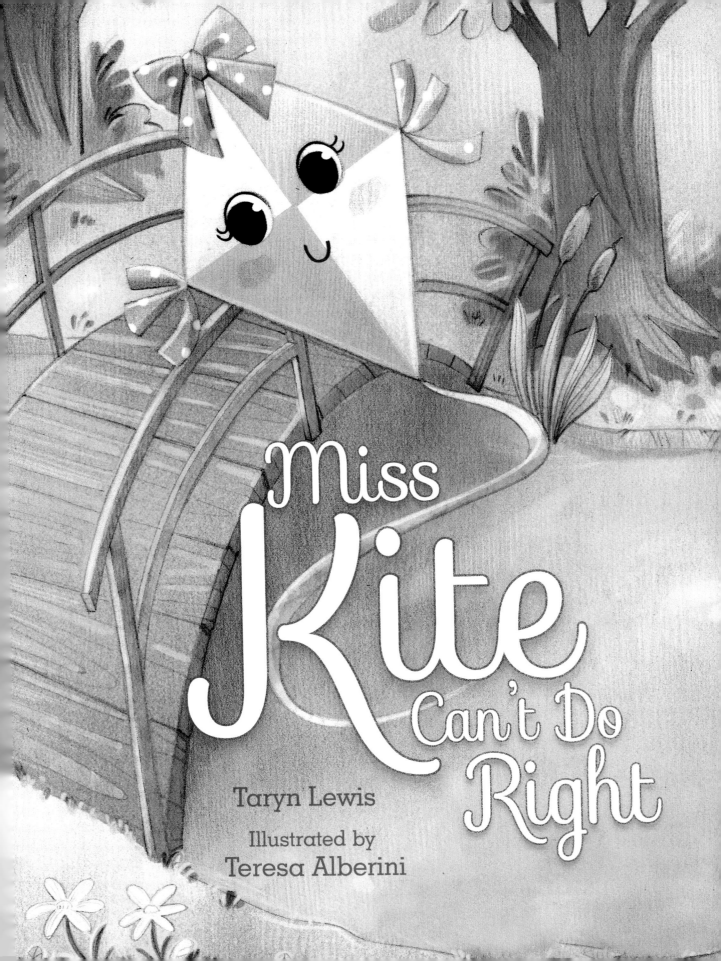

Miss Kite Can't Do Right

Taryn Lewis

Illustrated by
Teresa Alberini

Miss Kite woke up ready to start the day's adventure
in her tiny treehouse apartment.

Her home was neatly decorated with all her bows and
ribbons, and the walls were filled with photos from all
the places Miss Kite—who loved to explore—had visited.
She had so many bows and ribbons that deciding which
one to wear was always the hardest part of her morning.

"I can't wait to see what today's adventures will bring," said Miss Kite as she flew out the door, having finally decided to wear her favorite polka-dot bow and striped ribbons.

OH! WHAT A BEAUTIFUL, SUNNY DAY.

It's the perfect day to go for a flight, thought Miss Kite.

But where should I go?

The playground,

the zoo,

the park,

or maybe a farm . . .

So many places to choose from . . . I know! I'll go to them all!

Miss Kite floated along and decided to stop at the playground, where she saw Ezra Elephant sitting on the swings, curled up in a ball.

"HELP ME!" cried Ezra.

Miss Kite floated down to help,
giving Ezra Elephant a BIG PUSH.

"WHEEE!"

said Miss Kite as Ezra
flew up in the air.

I SURE AM BEING HELPFUL . . .

she thought.

Ezra yelled, "No, you weren't listening! I didn't want to swing. I was sitting here because I'm scared of that mouse!"

But Miss Kite had already floated off to her next stop. She wasn't listening.

Miss Kite was floating along when she spotted a zoo in the distance, where she saw Allie Alpaca standing by a fence with a half-smile, half-frown on her face.

"HELP ME!" cried Allie.

Miss Kite floated down to help as she got out her camera, thinking about how great a picture of Allie Alpaca would look in her photo album.

"SAY CHEESE!" said Miss Kite as Allie stood there. *I sure am being helpful,* she thought.

Allie yelled, "No, you weren't listening! I didn't need my picture taken. I am standing here because my fur is stuck in the fence!"

But Miss Kite had already floated off to her next stop. She wasn't listening.

As Miss Kite flew along, she decided to stop at the park, where she saw Tobias Turtle flipped upside down onto his shell.

"HELP ME!" cried Tobias.

Miss Kite floated down to help, giving Tobias Turtle a fluffy pillow to rest his head on.

"WHAT A QUIET PLACE FOR A NAP,"

said Miss Kite as she placed the pillow under Tobias Turtle's head. *I sure am being helpful,* she thought.

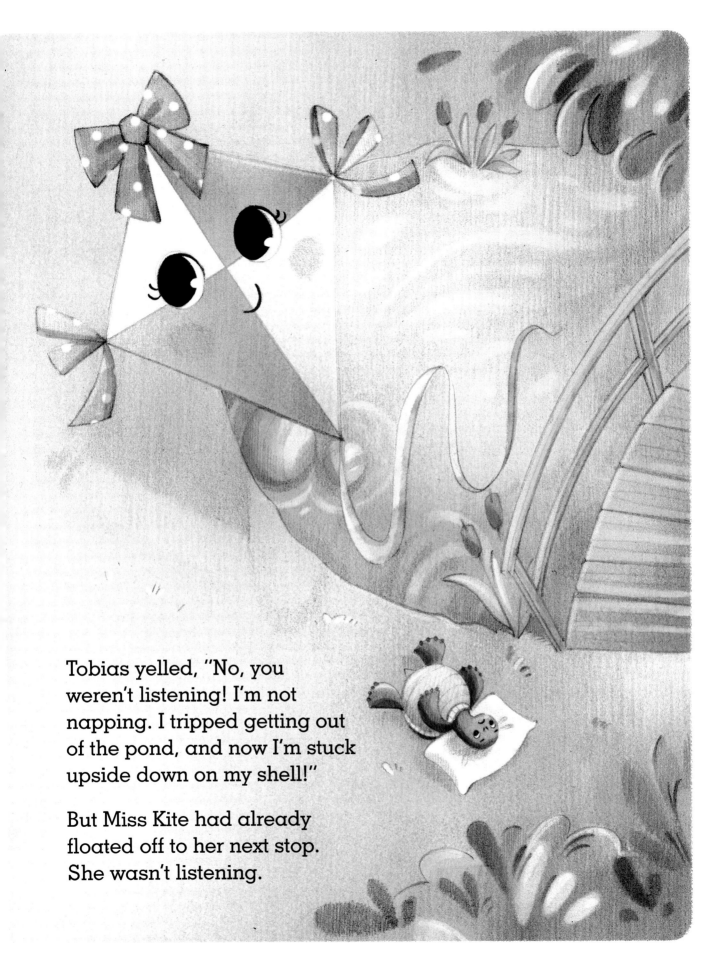

Tobias yelled, "No, you weren't listening! I'm not napping. I tripped getting out of the pond, and now I'm stuck upside down on my shell!"

But Miss Kite had already floated off to her next stop. She wasn't listening.

The day was almost done, and the sun was setting. Miss Kite was heading home when she floated by a farm, where she saw Hollyn Horse standing up on her tippy toes.

"HELP ME!" cried Hollyn.

Miss Kite floated down to help, giving Hollyn Horse a tutu to help with her ballet dancing.

"BRAVO! WHAT A WONDERFUL DANCE!"

said Miss Kite, clapping for Hollyn Horse. *I sure am being helpful,* she thought.

Hollyn yelled, "No, you weren't listening! I'm not dancing. I'm trying to reach the apples in the tree because I'm hungry!"

But Miss Kite had already floated off toward home. She wasn't listening.

Miss Kite got ready for bed, thinking about all the good deeds she had done that day and the new friends she had made.

I sure am good at being helpful, she thought as she tucked herself into bed and turned out the light.

The next day, Miss Kite heard a knock on her door. It was all her new friends coming to visit:

EZRA ELEPHANT,
   ALLIE ALPACA,
      TOBIAS TURTLE,
         AND HOLLYN HORSE.

"You were not very helpful yesterday. You didn't listen to what we were saying!" said Miss Kite's new friends.

"You floated away before we could finish asking for help," said Tobias Turtle.

Miss Kite was sad that her friends were upset with her. She hadn't realized that when she didn't fully listen to her friends and what they needed, she wasn't being helpful.

"I'M SO SORRY," said Miss Kite. "I didn't realize I wasn't listening."

"It's okay, Miss Kite. We just want to help you be a better friend, starting with listening," said Hollyn Horse.

WOW, thought Miss Kite. *That sure was helpful . . . and I just had to listen to what my friends had to say!*

Miss Kite promised her new friends that she would be a better friend and listener.

She invited them all to sit down to enjoy a cup of tea, making sure to ask each friend just how they liked it before fixing their cups:

two lumps of sugar for Ezra Elephant,

a dash of milk, for Allie Alpaca,

a drop of honey for Tobias Turtle,

and a little bit of everything for Hollyn Horse.

WHAT A BEAUTIFUL DAY,

thought Miss Kite as she joined them at the table.
It's the perfect day to spend with friends.

ABOUT THE
AUTHOR

Taryn lives in Virginia with her husband, Dermaine, and their daughter, Morgan. Before she started writing children's books, Taryn earned her degree in Business Administration from the University of Mary Washington. Writing a children's book has always been a dream for Taryn, and when the pandemic hit, she decided to fulfill that dream! When Taryn's not writing stories, she's working her 9–5 in the insurance regulatory industry.